Janice Woodhams
from S. S. teacher
Mr. Allen Law
June – 1964

BEVERLY'S QUEST

OTHER BOOKS BY THE SAME AUTHOR —

Together We'll Do It

Just for Girls

Just for Mothers

Medical Missionaries You Would Like to Know

Twice-Born Stars You Would Like to Know

BEVERLY'S QUEST

A Modern Girl's Search for Truth and Happiness

by
DOROTHY C. HASKIN

ZONDERVAN PUBLISHING HOUSE
GRAND RAPIDS, MICHIGAN

Printed in the United States of America

CONTENTS

BEVERLY'S QUEST

1: "WEEPING FOR A NIGHT" (Psalm 30:5)

BEVERLY HARRIS PULLED NERVOUSLY at the bed covers, snuggled down another inch, and tried to be quiet as she worried, *I wish Jack would get home. He shouldn't have gone hot-rod racing with the boys. He says it's all right but if it were he'd have told Mom and Dad where he was going. He's real keen but too anxious to be friends with all the boys.*

She strained to hear the sound of the front door opening. *Of course Jack was right not to worry Mom, but* — A wave of sleepiness rolled over her and she drifted into unconsciousness only to be jerked to awareness by the shrill ringing of the phone. *Who can that be?* She lifted her head from the pillow, half-sitting up in bed. Mrs. Harris had answered and was talking in a high-pitched excited voice.

Bev jumped out of bed and opened the door to the hall. Mr. Harris grabbed the phone from his wife and began asking quick, terse questions.

"My boy! My boy!" Mrs. Harris sobbed.

Harris banged the phone in its cradle and in an agitated tone, shouted, "Mae, don't carry on like that! Jack will be all right!"

"What's wrong?" Bev asked, filled with fear for her brother.

9

"That was the Town Hospital. The boys were in a smash-up on Richmond Road, and they're all hurt."

"Take me to my boy! Take me to him!" Mrs. Harris cried.

"Of course, we'll go to him. Hurry and get dressed."

"I'm going with you," Bev called to her parents. *Jack can't be too hurt,* her heart insisted but her mind reminded, *But he is!* She put on her skirt and sweater. She was standing in front of her dresser, giving her long blonde bob a quick brushing when Mrs. Harris in a flurried voice, called, "Bev, please come here."

Bev threw the brush on the dresser and stepped into the hall.

"I can't zip my zipper," Mrs. Harris fussed, rubbing her hands nervously together.

"I'll fix it." Bev tugged at the side zipper of her mother's dress.

"I'll get the car," Mr. Harris shouted as he crossed the living room, going out the front door.

By the time Bev had the zipper closed, had found her mother's purse and coat, and they had hurried down the stairs, Harris had the car waiting at the curb.

He streaked across the murky city. Bev thought how odd it was to see the street lights shining with all the houses so dark and quiet and the streets deserted. She had never been out late at night like this. The empty look of everything only increased her feeling of sadness. She thought, *Nothing serious must happen to Jack.*

She and Jack had been closer than many brothers

and sisters. There were only thirteen months between them and he was a part of her every memory. She even dimly remembered those early years when she didn't sense any difference between Jack and herself, when they were both just children. Then, he'd grown a little older and she had realized that he was a boy! How sad she had felt when he wanted to play with the gang instead of with her! But sometimes he got mad at his friends and came back to her for comfort. Too, he had been proud of her because she was pretty. There'd been a real closeness between them — she was, in a way, closer to him than she was to either her mother or father. Ofttimes, like tonight, he had confided in her when he hadn't in his parents.

She was proud of him, his thick chestnut hair and quick, warm smile. All the girls were crazy about him! He enjoyed being popular. That was why he'd gone with the boys tonight to Richmond Road.

There'd been a sense in which he hadn't wanted to go with the boys. He had said it was the last Saturday he was going out with them. He knew they didn't always do the right things. That was because he'd begun going to church of late. Some months ago one of his friends had invited Jack to go with him. Lately, Jack had been going to church more and more often. Even by himself. He'd been changing about things, too. About the way he looked at cheating and driving too fast. Church meant a lot to him.

He'd even persuaded Bev to go a couple of times with him but she hadn't known any of the girls, except Grace Grant. And Bev didn't know Grace too well. So Bev hadn't gone again. Jack had felt real bad about her not going. Now she wished she'd gone. *It would have made him happy. He was sort of excited about what he believed. I wish I knew what I believed about God and stuff like that.*

With a sudden swerve that made Bev grip the car door, her father drove into the parking lot of the sprawling hospital and parked. There were only half a dozen cars on the big lot. It felt chilly as they hurried into the quiet hospital to a nurse at the front desk. In a "I-must-be-kind-though-I-am-busy" manner, the nurse waved toward a waiting room and explained, "Dr. Robb will see you as soon as he's free."

Bev and her parents went into the waiting room. With a feeling of dismay Bev glanced at the worn divan and the magazines, lying askew on the table, as if the reader had been called away hurriedly.

Bev and Mrs. Harris sat on the divan while Mr. Harris nervously paced from the window to the table and back to the window. Her mother cried silently, dabbing her eyes with a damp tissue, and Bev thought, *I want to see Jack now,* as if thinking it would make it come true.

There was a stir in the hall. Bev looked up and in came the Graysons and the Pattons. *The parents of the other boys!* Everyone began talking at the same time, trying to tell each other what little they had heard of the accident.

Then Mrs. Grayson half collapsed on the divan, weeping loudly in her husband's large, white handkerchief. Mrs. Patton dropped quietly onto a chair and Bev thought, *I wish she'd cry too. She looks so tense, with the cords of her neck stretched stiff like that!*

Mrs. Patton kept muttering over and over again, "Clyde looked so good when he left the house. So good! Tall and straight. I was so proud of him. So proud!"

The men stood in the doorway, talking in jerky sentences. First Mr. Grayson would stare anxiously down the hall, then Mr. Patton, and then Mr. Harris. At times, they'd stop talking and all stare down the hall.

It's a nightmare, Bev thought.

"Here comes Dr. Robb!" exclaimed Harris.

Bev and the mothers jumped up, hurrying to the door. The doctor, a portly man with a pleasant smile, came toward them. "The boys are alive and right now, that's the main thing. Apparently no concussions, but, as to be expected, shock and bruises. And Clyde's arm is broken."

"My poor boy!" Mrs. Patton exclaimed.

"I've set it and it will heal. Otherwise, it will be sometime tomorrow before I'm certain of the extent of the boys' injuries. You may see them for a few moments, then go home and get some sleep."

They followed Dr. Robb down the hall, saw briefly the boys who were under sedation, and then there was nothing to do but leave. In the parking lot Mrs. Harris begged her friends, "If you hear anything let me know."

"Yes, and you, too," Mrs. Grayson answered.

"We'll keep each other informed," Mrs. Patton promised.

The Harrises got into their car and as they drove toward home Bev saw that dawn was coming like a lagging child into the city. The street lights had been turned out and a faint haze covered the city. Now and then a bus drove noisily by. Occasionally a man, carrying a lunch box, walked slowly down the street. Everything looked as gray and dreary as Bev's heart felt.

All over the week end Bev's heart felt heavy, and it was not until Monday morning that the doctor let her and her parents stay a few minutes by Jack's bed. He was so still and white, but he did open his brown eyes and seem to recognize them. And that helped.

Back in the hall Dr. Robb looked professional and earnest as he told them, "Andy Grayson suffered merely shock and bruises and has gone home. Clyde Patton's arm is in a cast and it will be sometime before he can use it."

"And Jack?" asked Mr. Harris in an insistent, anxious tone.

"We expect he will recover but we have to watch so that infection and possibly blood poisoning does not set in. He cut his hand badly, apparently on the broken windshield."

"Yes," Harris agreed, "those old cars don't have the new shatter proof kind."

"I cleaned the wound but it was so swollen and ragged that I'm not certain I cleaned out all the infective material. I want to keep him under observation for a few days."

More waiting! Bev knew she just couldn't wait

any longer. Waiting was the hardest thing in the world to do.

The Harrises were troubled by the doctor's report and said little on the way home but when they reached their apartment Harris decided, "We might as well be sensible. There is nothing we can do but wait, so tomorrow, Bev, you're going back to school."

"School! I couldn't stand it!"

"I said you were going and I meant it!"

Bev hesitated. Should she argue with her father? She knew that if she pleaded and fussed she could probably have her own way. He always blustered at first but if she or her mother persisted, he'd give in. *Still, with Jack hurt I don't have the heart to argue with Dad. And maybe he's right. Maybe I would feel better if I were busy!*

The next morning the family followed its regular routine of hurry, hurry, trying to get out of the house on time. Bev kept missing Jack. He always fussed over the length of time she spent in the bathroom, but he did walk to school with her, talking to her about her math or whatever was bothering her. It was hard to be alone.

She sat forlornly through the morning classes, then at noon she went to her locker for her lunch and found she had forgotten to bring it. She closed her locker door and leaned against it with a gone feeling, not wanting to eat anyway.

Grace Grant, who had the locker next to Bev's, asked, "Forget your lunch?"

"Yes, but it doesn't matter. With Jack hurt, nothing matters."

Grace put her arm around Bev's shoulder and in a comforting tone, said, "I read about the accident in the paper and know you must feel terrible. Come on, we'll share my lunch."

Bev followed Grace out of the locker room into the school yard. The sun was shining and the girls were sitting around in little groups, eating and laughing. Bev and Grace found a place on the "Aud" steps.

"Was he badly hurt?" Grace asked.

"That's the awful part! The doctor doesn't tell us anything certain and I can't stand to wait."

"Here, have a sandwich. Mom always gives me too much." Grace passed Bev a sandwich.

Bev munched the thinly sliced bread and pimento cheese. It did taste better than she had expected. Maybe because there were little tart bits of pickle in it.

It was sweet of Grace to share with her. Grace wasn't really one of her close friends. She was pretty in a way but her hair was sort of sandy colored and her blue eyes were small. But she was always cheerful. Not that Bev knew of anything special Grace had to make her happy. She didn't have near the amount of clothes that some of her friends, like Thelma and Nadine, did.

Besides, Grace was too religious to suit Bev. Grace was always talking about the Lord! She went to the same church that Jack had been going to. But maybe if she talked to Grace about Jack, Grace would pray for him. People were always saying that prayer helped. Bev began, "Maybe you can help. That is, if you'll ——"

"Hi," came an unexpected voice.

Bev glanced up at Thelma Brooks and Nadine Lockwood. Sometimes Thelma and Nadine were thick. Again, they didn't speak for days. It was really odd that they were friends, they were so different. Thelma was a real smart looking girl with hair that was the prettiest shade of auburn, like an autumn leaf. And she wore real keen clothes. Her green suede jacket looked as if her dad had paid plenty for it. Nadine was pretty too, with real black hair. She didn't have Thelma's smartness. She wore a black and white plaid skirt and a red checked blouse that looked loud together.

Grace glanced at the girls, put her arm around Bev's shoulder and gave her a squeeze, saying, "Bev's upset about her brother."

"I heard about it. I'm sorry," Nadine said with geninue interest.

A slight frown crossed Thelma's face and in an airy tone she said, "If she holds the right thought he'll get well."

How can a thought help Jack get well when even the doctor doesn't know how seriously he's hurt? Bev wondered.

"He was in a crack-up on Richmond Road," Grace added.

"So what! I know how he can be healed."

"How?" Bev demanded, excited at the idea of Jack's being well again.

"Through Science. Christian Science that is," Thelma answered.

Bev tried to think of everything she had ever

heard about Christian Science but she really didn't know except that it was some sort of a religion.

"If you girls are going to talk Science, don't let me stop you, but I'm more interested in my own brand of religion," Nadine said as she walked away from the girls.

"She's prejudiced," Thelma explained with a superior air.

"Well, maybe I am too," Grace admitted, "but I don't see how Christian Science can help Jack."

"And what, may I ask, do you know about Science?"

"Nothing much," Grace admitted, sort of backing down. "Only what Pastor Lynch says, and he says it's a cult."

"Ministers don't know everything and you shouldn't go only by what you hear. You should find out for yourself. Though I must say, Bev's brother is no concern of mine, if she doesn't care to claim him as God's perfect child." Thelma turned to walk away.

"Wait!" Bev jumped up, grabbing Thelma's arm. "If Christian Science will help Jack, I've got to know about it."

"But Bev, it won't. It's wrong," Grace objected.

"Science is one of the latest advancements mankind has made," Thelma answered, the usually quiet girl growing enthusiastic. "It teaches that 'all is infinite Mind' and 'matter is mortal error' and that 'sickness is a belief, which must be annihilated by the Divine Mind.' "*

* See note at back of book.

"You mean that Jack really isn't sick?" Bev tried to grasp what her friend was trying to say.

"Yes, sickness is mortal error and you must deny error."

Bev wanted to ask what "error" was but before she could, Grace interrupted, "But what does your Christian Science teach about the Lord Jesus Christ?"

"That He was the way-shower," Thelma explained, in a tone that showed that she was being very patient.

"No, He *is* the Way," Grace insisted.

And which one, Bev wondered, was right!

2: "GREAT, SWELLING WORDS" (II Peter 2:18)

THAT AFTERNOON DURING CLASS, Bev scarcely listened to Miss Mackintosh explain to the class about the culture of Mexico. Instead, she filled a sheet of paper with sketches of wrecked autos and wondered, *Can Christian Science make Jack well and strong again?* She knew so little of religion.

Her grandmother Harris went to church but she lived so far away. And her parents had both gone to church when they were younger, but since they had moved to this larger city, and had the two babies so close together, they had stopped going. If only she had gone more when Jack wanted her to go, then she'd know if Grace or Thelma were right, and if the Christian Science could help Jack. *I've just got to find out if it can!*

As soon as the last bell rang, Bev started toward Thelma. Someone touched her arm. Bev glanced over her shoulder. Grace's small, oval face was serious as she offered, "Bev, I'll pray for your brother."

"Thank you," Bev said as politely as she could, but she was more anxious to speak to Thelma. She pulled away, hurrying after the flash of auburn hair that disappeared through the door. It was good-hearted of Grace to say she'd pray, but Thelma had promised that Christian Science would heal!

Thelma was half-way across the school grounds before Bev caught up with her. Excitedly she demanded, "Please tell me all about Christian Science."

"If you walk with me I'll tell you what I can. Otherwise, I can't waste my time."

Bev clung to Thelma's arm and walked beside her.

"The best I can say is that I've gone to the Science Church ever since I can remember and I've never been sick."

Bev nodded but she thought, *I want proof. Thelma's not being sick isn't positive proof that Christian Science keeps people well for I haven't been sick much.* "Haven't you even had colds?"

"Sometimes mortal error has tried to manifest itself," Thelma admitted, almost reluctantly.

"You mentioned mortal error at noon. What is it?"

"It is really mortal mind. That is, 'Nothing claiming to be something, for Mind is immortal.' My Dad doesn't fool with mortal error. The minute it manifests itself, he makes me go to bed and phones our practitioner."

"What's a practitioner?"

"A man or woman who is advanced in the study of Science. You go to one of them for help when you can't make your own demonstration."

"What's a demonstration?"

"Goodness, how many questions you can ask!

Anyway, it's making whatever you think become a reality."

"I see," Bev answered, but she wasn't sure that she did. They had reached the brick apartment house where Bev lived, so she invited, "Won't you come up and tell Mom about Christian Science?"

Thelma glanced down the street toward her home. "I really don't have time, but I suppose I ought to."

"Oh, thanks a lot!" Bev led Thelma up the stairs and into the Harris's apartment. Mrs. Harris was sitting on the corner of the divan, crying. Fear for her brother filled Bev as she ran to her mother. "Is Jack worse?"

Mrs. Harris lifted her head and dabbed her eyes. "No, that is, not that I know of, but the doctor won't tell me anything definite and I'm worried sick."

"You don't need to worry any more," Bev said happily. "Thelma knows something that will make Jack well."

"What?"

"She'll tell you." Bev dropped beside her Mom on the divan and waved for Thelma to sit down. Thelma sat on a straight chair, arched her eyebrows and in an adult manner, said, "If you will study Science, you will have no more trouble with mortal error. Our family has always believed in Science and we make our demonstrations."

"She means Christian Science," Bev explained.

"How? Tell me!" Mrs. Harris asked excitedly.

"Really, I'm only a student of Science. Let me loan you my copy of 'Science and Health' and I'll get you our practitioner, Mrs. Blackwell's, number. She'll help you."

"That's sweet of you!"

"And now I've got to go."

Bev was disappointed because Thelma wouldn't stay longer. She wanted to know everything that very instant so Jack wouldn't be sick another moment. But when Thelma said no she could be very stubborn.

Bev walked to the head of the stairs with her friend, then hurried back to her mother and tried to explain what Thelma had told her about Christian Science. She added, "You see, everything is in one's mind, and if you think right, why, everything *is* all right."

The phone rang. Bev glanced at it impatiently. *Who's calling now?* She waved to her mother that she would answer it, and did, in an irritated tone, saying, "Hello."

"Hello," answered a friendly voice at the other end. "This is Pastor Lynch. I just heard that your brother had been in an accident, and I wondered if I could go see him, or do anything for you folks."

Some minister! How could he help! Bev thought and answered, "I'm sorry. Jack's too sick to see anyone, and I don't know anything you could do for us."

"You know, Jack has been attending our church of late so I'd be glad to do anything to help."

So that's who he is! "Thank you but there isn't anything you can do," Bev repeated and felt relieved when he hung up.

All she was interested in was the idea that Christian Science could heal her brother. *What if the church promises that much?* She remembered vaguely that she had heard of divine healers but she didn't know anything about them and she could know about Science, if only Thelma kept her word!

She was anxious all that evening and the next morning. But, at school, during the first period, Thelma waved a black book at Bev and she felt relieved. *That must be it! She has brought it!*

She sat through classes with sort of a suppressed excitement until lunch period, then, out on the "Aud" steps, Thelma gave the copy of "Science and Health" to Bev. Full of curiosity Bev opened and on the first page read, "There is nothing either good or bad, but thinking makes it so — Shakespeare."

That was what Thelma had been saying — sickness was nothing. The first chapter was on "Prayer." That ought to be easy to understand, but she certainly wondered what the fifth chapter "Animal Magnetism Unmasked" could be about.

After school, Bev insisted that Thelma go home with her. Bev and her mother sat on the divan while Thelma read to them from the chapter on "Science, Theology, Medicine." Bev wished she understood it better but too many of the words were new to her, such as: "Apodictical Principle" — "feeling so perpetually the false consciousness that life inheres in the body" — and "matter possesses neither sensation nor life."

She felt as if she were walking through a thick mist. Only by asking Thelma question after question did she understand that she must never say that Jack was sick, because it was only mortal error which made him appear as if he were sick. He really was not sick. He was God's perfect child. Bev sighed, "He looks so sick!"

"And so pale and drawn," Mrs. Harris said in a frightened tone.

"If you want him to be well, you must practice the truth," Thelma rebuked in a superior tone. "If you as much as think he is sick, then it is your fault if he doesn't get well."

"Read some more," Bev encouraged. *I'll just have to learn to control my thoughts.*

"No, you can read to yourself. And phone Mrs. Blackwell, she'll help you. I don't have the time."

"Yes, do, Mom. Maybe we can see her tomorrow after school."

Thelma waited while Mrs. Harris phoned and made her appointment, then she left. Bev curled up on the divan and continued reading "Science and Health." But it was full of sentences such as: "To develop the full might of this Science, the discords of corporeal sense must yield to the harmony of spiritual sense." Bev wondered if this could be the double talk people joked about, but instantly felt guilty because she had thought such a thing.

The hope of the coming interview with the practitioner sustained her all that evening and the next day at school. When she came home, she almost felt her old self, she was so hopeful about Jack. He would soon be lumbering up the stairs, slamming the door, laughing loudly. And when he knew all that Science had done for him, he'd be glad to change churches, and this time, she'd go with him. She hummed as she

changed into a fresh pink blouse. By that time Mrs.
Harris was dressed in the brown suit and small hat
that she usually wore when she went shopping.

They took the bus the short distance to the downtown district, to the big building where Mrs. Blackwell's office was located. It was only one room, fur-
nished with a thick rug, easy chairs and a gray-shaded
standing lamp.

"Beverly's dear friend, Thelma Brooks, told us
about you," Mrs. Harris began.

"I know the Brooks' family," Mrs. Blackwell
nodded with a polite smile.

"We're in deep trouble." Mrs. Harris lowered
her voice as she talked of Jack, how much he meant
to them, and the accident.

Mrs. Blackwell listened with a calm, almost expressionless face. She reminded Bev of Thelma. *Of
course, Mrs. Blackwell is stout and has gray hair, but
she has that same manner, as if she were afraid error
might touch her. Scientists seem to act as if they are
above sympathizing with other people's troubles. Maybe that's because they know we bring on our troubles
by being afraid.*

"He's dreadfully ill! The doctor says ———"

Mrs. Blackwell lifted her hand, silencing Mrs.
Harris, "Please don't tell me what the doctor says,
that is only voicing error."

"Do you think Christian Science can heal my son?"

"To quote 'Science and Health,' 'Erroneous belief
is destroyed by truth.' The truth will heal your son
of his erroneous belief."

Those big words again! Bev translated them,

Jack will get well. That was what she wanted to happen and so did her Mom! She leaned over and squeezed Mrs. Harris' hand.

"I never refuse to treat anyone," Mrs. Blackwell continued, "but I guarantee no results as long as he is surrounded by error which may counteract the good I am affirming."

Bev could almost see Mrs. Blackwell's thoughts, like white spears, fighting the black spears of the thoughts of the doctors and nurses. It was a battle of the minds, with Jack's very life at stake.

"I'll treat him now." Mrs. Blackwell bowed her head in her hands and was silent. Bev tried to affirm with her, *Jack is going to get well, Jack is going to get well!* She tried so hard that she grew tired and was relieved when Mrs. Blackwell looked up, the treatment over.

After a few more words, Mrs. Harris paid the practitioner, and Bev and her mother went into the hall. Bev anxiously asked, "Do you think she will help Jack?"

"I hope so," Mrs. Harris answered, "but we can't afford to go to her and also pay the doctor. The doctor is only letting Jack lie there, waiting to see if anything develops. I think I'll speak to your Dad about bringing Jack home."

Bring Jack home! The very idea made it sound as if he were better already! Happily Bev exclaimed, "We must!"

"We'll see what Dad says tonight."

"Oh!" Bev hesitated. She knew her father. He didn't like the family making decisions without him.

That was one reason why Jack hadn't told him where he was going the night he was hurt. But, too, her dad could be won around, so she suggested, "Tell him after dinner."

"And I'll fix exactly what he likes."

"Do," Bev nodded, knowing that was a concession on her mother's part. Her parents didn't really like the same things to eat. Mrs. Harris always enjoyed fancy casserole dishes while Mr. Harris was a meat and potato man.

But that night for dinner they had Salisbury steak, crisp French Fried potatoes, and the only vegetable that Mr. Harris really liked, stewed tomatoes.

For dessert Mrs. Harris had bought a frozen apple pie and baked it. When they began eating the pie, Mrs. Harris couldn't contain herself any longer but began telling her husband about the visit to the practitioner. Before she was finished, Harris interrupted, "I don't think it will work. The doctor knows his business."

"Doctors don't know everything." Mrs. Harris dropped her fork and leaned anxiously across the table, "Didn't you tell me that once a doctor gave your mother up to die and she was healed?"

"That was different," he objected. "It had nothing to do with Christian Science. Only, plain old-fashioned faith in God." He squinted his blue eyes wistfully and added, "I wish I had Mom's faith."

Bev wasn't interested in all this discussion of her grandmother's faith but in Jack, so she broke in, "Mrs. Blackwell won't promise to help Jack as long as he's at the hospital, so Mom and I think we ought to bring him home."

"You know the doctor won't dismiss him."

"But, Dad ———" she began.

Her mother nodded for her not to talk, and directed, "Clear the table, Bev." Bev picked up the empty pie plates and walked with them into the kitchen while Mrs. Harris began arguing and pleading with Mr. Harris. Their voices grew louder and louder, until in a desperate tone, Mrs. Harris cried. "But he's your only son. I'd think you'd do anything to help him."

"All right, all right," Harris exclaimed exasperated and Bev knew that her mother had won the argument. She stepped to the door and listened while her father finished, "Bring him home, if you must have your way. The doctor has probably done all he can and the Christian Science won't kill him. And at least we'll have a little peace around here."

Bev ran to him, threw her arms around his neck and kissed his cheek. "Dad, you're a dear."

As soon as Bev and Mrs. Harris were in the kitchen, doing dishes, they began planning. Mr. Harris didn't earn a large enough salary for Jack to have his own room. He slept on the divan in the living room and kept his clothes in his parents' closet. Bev and her mother decided that he could have Bev's room. She offered, "I'll sleep on the divan and be glad to."

The next day she stayed home from school to help her mother. She moved her toilet articles into the bathroom while Mrs. Harris talked to the doctor on the phone.

Bev, half-listening, could tell her mother was arguing with him. Finally, she hung up and in a frightened voice said, "He says if we take Jack from the hospital, we'll have to take the full responsibility for whatever happens to him."

"But we can't just leave him there. Phone the practitioner," Bev suggested, upset because things weren't going smoothly.

Mrs. Harris called Mrs. Blackwell, and when she finished talking to her she looked happier. "She suggested that the doctor might be willing if we agree to bring Jack home in an ambulance, and if so, she will treat him while he is on the way."

"I hope so! But isn't using an ambulance compromising with error?" Bev was surprised that the practitioner even suggested such a thing! She was pleased at her grasp of Science, but, too, this was no time to argue with anyone. *The important thing is to get Jack home!* She encouraged, "You'd better phone and see what Dr. Robb says to that."

Mrs. Harris phoned the suggestion to the doctor, and he reluctantly agreed. After making several more calls, Mrs. Harris had everything arranged. Bev floated happily around the apartment, trying to think of everything she could to make Jack comfortable, turning down the bed, fluffing up the pillows, putting his recorder into the bedroom.

Within two hours, the attendants carried Jack into the apartment on a stretcher and helped Mrs. Harris settle him into the bedroom. It seemed wonderful to have him home! Except that it distressed Bev to see his face so white and his lips so pale. His only color was his thick brown hair and a redness on his wrist above the bandage.

Bev's fingers itched to yank off the bandage. *It is error!* She clenched her fists and determined, "I'll work that Science if ever anyone worked it. Jack's got to be well again."

Jack couldn't be sick. He was too full of laughter and eagerness. He was willing to try again. That was because he was full of life! She'd get him that way again, by her thinking. Over and over she affirmed. *Jack is well. Jack is perfect. All is infinite mind. Sickness is mortal belief.* It was like a chant that if she said it often enough, Jack would be well.

3: "THINGS TO COME" (John 16:13)

THE NEXT DAY, AFTER SCHOOL, Bev walked home with Thelma and excitedly told her about Jack's being home.

"That's good," Thelma said with a warmer smile than usual, "and do you mind if I stop by at your place and get my copy of 'Science and Health'?"

"No," Bev answered, but she was sorry to give up the book. It was so important that she know everything possible about Christian Science so that Jack would get well soon. But it was Thelma's book so when they reached her apartment house, she ran upstairs and brought the book down to Thelma.

"Thanks a million," Thelma said and went swinging down the street.

Bev watched her wistfully for a moment. *Thelma seems so happy. And, of course, it is this wonderful Christian Science that makes her happy!* She sighed, then hurried upstairs to help her mother take care of Jack. There wasn't too much she could do. Just sit by Jack's bed and not let herself worry when he moaned.

Back at school, Friday noon, as she sat on the bench on the shady side of the school building, she

32

wished Thelma would come talk to her. Instead, Grace sat down beside her.

"Hi." Grace took off her rose-colored sweater and laid it across her lap. With a concerned look, she asked, "Did Thelma talk any more to you about Christian Science?"

"Yes, and what's more, we've brought Jack home from the hospital and Science is going to heal him," Bev said flatly, not daring to express the fear that was in the depth of her heart.

"Only God, not Christian Science, can heal anyone," Grace hotly corrected. "I suppose I shouldn't butt in, but can't you see that Christian Science is a cult?"

"What's a 'cult'?" Beverly had heard the word but she wasn't sure what it meant.

"A cult is a religion that isn't a regular one. It's a phoney — one that's all wrong."

"How can you say that? Thelma says her family has always believed in Science and that it has helped them."

"It didn't help her mother. She died."

Bev felt her color leave her face. "What do you mean?"

"I mean her mother died. You ask her. Thelma lives with her Dad and older sister. Mrs. Brooks was sick for nearly a year. I know because Mom used to go see her and try to help her, but she clung to that Christian Science. And when Mrs. Brooks died, Thelma and her family acted as if nothing had happened."

Hope seeped out of Beverly's heart. She stared at the toe of her brown oxford. *Suppose Christian*

Science doesn't heal Jack? Suppose ——— She mustn't think such things! She lifted her face, "I'll ask Thelma about it."

Thelma, she knew, would explain her mother's death and everything would be all right! She looked around for Thelma. But the bell rang and she had to go to classes. And after school Thelma disappeared before Bev could talk to her.

She planned to go to Thelma's house on Saturday, but she had to stay home and help her mother take care of Jack. Every time he moaned, as he did more and more frequently, Bev thought of Mrs. Brooks' dying. She didn't tell her Mom about the Scientist's death because she didn't want her to be upset. Besides, it wasn't fair to say anything until she heard Thelma's explanation.

She had been so hopeful that as soon as Jack was home, under Mrs. Blackwell's treatment, he would be his old, happy self. It hurt to see him lie in a queer sleep like a stupor, twisting and thrashing in the bed. Occasionally her Mom was able to get him to sip some water or hot broth. But mostly he just lay there on the bed.

Perhaps, she thought, *hearing his records would help.* With renewed hope she went over to Jack's record player on the dresser and glanced through his stack of records.

The top one was "It Took a Miracle." *One of his newest ones. A religious one. But that's right for now. We need a miracle!* She put it on and listened intensely to the sweet voice of the singer:

It took a miracle to put the stars in place,
It took a miracle to hang the world in space
But when He saved my soul, cleansed and made me whole,
It took a miracle of love and grace.

It's pretty, but I'd better get our miracle work-ing. She went into the kitchen where Mrs. Harris was studying the section on Invalid Cookery in her cookbook. She looked up and Bev reminded, "Mom, didn't Mrs. Blackwell say something about studying the lesson?"

"Yes," Mrs. Harris nodded.

"Then shouldn't we do it? Don't you think we ought to do everything we can?"

"Yes, Bev. You are right. After lunch, I'll go to the Scientist's reading room and buy a 'Science and Health' and whatever else we need."

"Oh, swell, Mom, swell!"

Hopeful once more, Bev went back into Jack's room and started his record again. When Mrs. Harris called her to lunch, she urged her mother to hurry and afterwards stood around trying to help while her mother dressed. It seemed as if Mrs. Harris were gone the longest time, but finally about three o'clock she got back from downtown with the "Science and Health" and a quarterly.

While waiting for her mother to take off her hat, Bev moved two chairs close to Jack's bedside, and, opening the quarterly, began studying it. She found the right day. Then, startled, realized, "Oh, Mom, we have to have a Bible too!"

Mrs. Harris stood in the doorway, frowning. "We have that old fine print Bible of Mother's but I don't remember where I put it. Maybe I can find it, but I simply can't afford to buy another thing."

Bev turned to glance at Jack, a frantic feeling mounting within her. They had to have a Bible! They had to study the lesson! Then she remembered, "Maybe I can borrow a Bible from Grace."

"Do try."

Bev pushed by Mrs. Harris into the hall and dialed her friend's number. When Grace answered, she asked, "I wonder if you have an extra Bible around the house. We need one, and———"

"Sure, Bev. I'll loan you mine and use Mom's. I'll bring it over."

"Thanks a lot." She put the receiver back on its cradle, exclaiming happily, "That Grace is super!"

In less than half an hour, Grace arrived with an almost new-looking Bible. There was a hopeful smile on her oval face as she explained, "It was a birthday present, but I'm glad to loan it to you."

"Thanks lots." Bev fingered the soft leather. *It is sweet of Grace to let me borrow it.*

"How's Jack?"

"He's better," she answered but inwardly she fretted, *Perhaps the reason I think Jack looks so bad is because I see him all the time and don't notice the change.* "Do you want to peek at him?"

"May I?"

Bev led her to the doorway. Grace stared at Jack, her face growing sad. When she stepped back into the living room, she said, slowly, "His skin is almost gray, isn't it?"

"Don't say such things!" Bev snapped. It bothered her that Grace, too, noticed how ill he looked!

"I'm sorry, I didn't mean anything wrong. And Bev, read lots of the Bible, won't you? Read the Gospels."

Bev nodded. She wondered what part of the Bible the Gospels were, but she wouldn't ask Grace and let her know how dumb she was.

After Grace left, Bev and her Mom studied the Science lesson and Bev wondered how anyone could ever read much of the Bible. She had trouble enough even finding the verses the quarterly said to read. The Bible was a strange book, full of queer names like Haggai and Malachi, and thee and thou language, which no one spoke any more. But then "Science and Health" seemed strange too. *Why does religion have to be so hard to understand?*

Despite the difficulties, Bev's love for her brother made her persistent, and Sunday, she and Mrs. Harris went to the Christian Science church. It was a square building, looking more like a public building than a church. Inside, the people were all well-dressed but seemed more business-like than worshipful.

While the readers in the pulpit read the same lesson Bev had studied at home, she, full of curiosity, glanced around. Painted in gold letters on one side of the front wall was: "Ye shall know the truth and the truth shall make you free. Jesus Christ." On the opposite side was: "Spirit is the only substance, the invisible and indivisible infinite God. Things spiritual and eternal are substantial. Things material and temporal are insubstantial. Mary Baker Eddy."

Evidently they thought the words of Jesus Christ and Mary Baker Eddy were of equal importance. Bev could picture Grace's look of shock if she told her that. Why, Grace thought there was no one, simply no one like the Lord! After she had looked at everything she could, Bev sat there bored. *The service part just isn't very interesting.*

At home, dinner was a quiet, worried meal, and afterwards, while her Mom and Dad discussed expenses, Bev sat by Jack's bedside. Occasionally she rubbed his forehead with her soft hand. He shook off her hand fretfully. His skin felt hot and feverish and that bothered her.

From the front room she could hear her Dad complain because he had to pay the practitioner for treating Jack each day. He objected, "And she doesn't even come to the house."

"She says absent treatments do as much good," Mrs. Harris explained in a low tired voice.

"They may do her as much good, but I don't see where they do Jack any good."

Bev frowned. She didn't like to hear her Dad talk like that. *Doesn't he understand he mustn't voice error?*

She turned Jack's hand over, wishing she could change the bandage. It was getting soiled and — a cold fear swept through her. Up his arm ran a red streak! She hadn't noticed it before. Frantically she pushed up his pajama sleeve and stared at the red streak. Was he getting worse?

She mustn't think such error! She wondered if her mother had noticed it. But if she had, she wouldn't say anything about it. That's what Science taught them, to ignore this false evidence of the mind. That only gave error power! She dropped his hand, but now with nagging fear, she knew she had to speak to Thelma about her mother's death. If Science hadn't helped her, how could she depend upon it to help Jack?

The next day at school Bev was relieved when she saw Thelma. When the noon bell rang she hurried over and exclaimed, "Thelma, I must talk to you!"

Thelma looked at her coldly and agreed. "After I get my lunch."

Bev got her lunch out of her locker and joined Thelma on one of the benches in the yard. Thelma began eating a sandwich but Bev was too upset even to open her lunch box. "Thelma, tell me something, I'm worried. Grace says that Science didn't help your mother, that she died anyway."

Thelma turned pale, and tucked a wisp of auburn hair carefully in place before she answered, "I never talk about my mother's passing."

"Not even to me? But I have to know! We're risking Jack's life on what you told us about Science!"

"Our family has made other demonstrations, so that proves Science is right. That time we failed and though I don't like to talk about it, I will tell you what really happened. Dad allowed mortal error to influence him. He took mother to the hospital and she died there."

Bev felt suddenly sorry for Thelma and her Dad. How awful they must feel, knowing it was their fear which killed Mrs. Brooks!

"You simply must not listen to Grace. She voices mortal error," Thelma retorted as near anger as she ever allowed herself to be.

"You're right," Bev nodded with vigor. *I won't go near Grace. She's a dear but she doesn't understand higher truths.*

"And we mustn't voice error. Let's talk about something else."

Bev tried to think of something else to discuss and, recalling that Nadine who sometimes chummed with Thelma was absent, said "I wonder why Nadine isn't at school."

"It's her own fault. She has let herself be sick again."

"Oh!" So much error! It made Bev feel very brave to battle it. One has to be on the alert all the time. With the feeling she must be strong to fight, she opened her lunch box and ate her carrot strips first.

She felt satisfied with herself and the struggle she was making until after classes. Then Grace started down the aisle toward her. Bev hurried away from her but as she did, Grace's smile disappeared and she looked sad. Bev told herself, *I can't help it if I do hurt Grace. She would only want to sympathize with me and that would be to express error.* As Bev walked slowly home alone, she realized, *I'm getting cold toward others like Thelma and Mrs. Blackwell. But if I'm going to practice Science I have to be able to keep my mind free from wrong thoughts.*

At home she went into Jack's room where she and her mother studied the lesson as outlined in the

Christian Science quarterly. This time the verses were a little easier to find. At least, she knew where Genesis was.

Afterward, when her mother went into the kitchen, Bev found herself staring at Jack's injured hand and wrist. The remembrance of the red streak fascinated her. *Is it still there? Does it mean that he's getting worse?*

Impulsively she turned his hand over. His pajama sleeve was rumpled and rolled part way up. The red streak went as far as she remembered! She pushed up his sleeve — it went even higher! With fear mounting in her heart, she opened his pajama coat and saw the red streak disappear in his armpit. She shook Jack, but he acted as if he were drugged. And his skin was such a dull green-gray!

So frightened she felt nauseated, she hurried out of the room and leaned against the door. When would she learn to ignore mortal error! Then she remembered "The Scientific Statement of Being" that she had been trying to memorize, and, like a charm, to ward off evil, she repeated over and over, "All is infinite Mind. All is infinite Mind."

She relaxed and felt better. During dinner, she almost, but not quite, forgot the red streak. Two or three times she found herself staring through the open door of the bedroom, wishing she could see more of Jack's arm. She thought of mentioning it to her Mom, but her worried expression checked Bev. *I mustn't add to Mom's troubles.* And if she told her Dad, she knew he'd call the doctor at once and Dr. Robb had never promised that Jack would get well while Christian Science had. She must wait and give Science a little more time to work.

She and her mother took turns staying with Jack. During the early part of the evening she sat by his bedside, doing her homework. But it was hard to study with Jack so sick. Once she got up and put on his record, "It Took a Miracle." As she listened to it, she bowed her head and repeated over and over again, "There is going to be a miracle, there is, there is." She thought of evenings when Jack had helped her with her homework and made her feel good by saying the review was just what he needed. He could help a person and at the same time make them feel they were doing him a favor. *Oh, he's a dear — there just has to be a miracle!*

The next day at school it was a relief to see Nadine was back and to think of something besides Jack. She had always thought Nadine was pretty, with her black hair that was really black, and hazel eyes that sort of changed color when she talked. She was always so alive, but she was too thin. *I'm going to help her. I'm not going to let her be sick again. I'll tell her about Christian Science.*

At lunch period she took her lunch, went over to where Nadine was sitting, and welcomed, "Hi, I'm glad you're back."

"I'm glad to be. But the least damp weather and I'm down with a cold. Like Dad used to be."

Bev sat beside her and, with a condescending smile, said, "But you don't need to be. You could use Christian Science."

Nadine gave a short, hard laugh. "Don't tell me

about Science! When Dad was so very sick, we heard about it and tried it. When he died, we decided we had heard too late. For two years I tried it, but it didn't help me. Science seems to work if you're strong anyway. And when it doesn't work, you don't blame the Science, but your lack of understanding."

"Oh!" Beverly felt all her old fears tie themselves in a hard knot in her throat. This was the second death of a Scientist of which she'd heard!

4: "THE LAST ENEMY" (I Corinthians 15:26)

"WE'VE TRIED THEM ALL," Nadine continued. "Unity, Theosophy, Religious Science, Science of Mind, and Numerology. None of these religions that claim you can do everything with your mind work when you really need them." Nadine coughed and leaned forward to try to stop it.

Nadine's complete denial of the power of Christian Science made Beverly feel weak. If only she could go home this minute and see that Jack was all right — that the red streak wasn't dangerous!

"What we're really interested in right now is Spiritualism. That really has the answers."

"Yes, I'm sure you're right, only right now, I've got to get home," Bev excused and abruptly she got up, crossed the school grounds and walked rapidly down the street, toward home . . . toward Jack . . . toward . . . . She grew cold as she wondered, *Toward what?*

She hurried up the stairs, opened the door of the apartment and stopped short. Dr. Robb was standing in the center of the room. Her Mom was huddled on the divan with her Dad sitting beside her, his arm around her shoulders.

44

"I can't understand how you let the boy get into this condition," Dr. Robb exclaimed.

Mr. Harris, his faced lined by the strain of his son's illness, stared at the doctor and admitted, "It's my fault. I noticed how gray Jack looked but I thought as long as he stayed in bed, he can't be getting worse. I hated to say anything to Mae. She was so blindly sure this Christian Science would cure him."

"Christian Science," Dr. Robb shook his head gravely. "It grieves me to see another family deceived by it. It is a subtle religion, appealing to many because it promises health and prosperity."

"But ——" Mrs. Harris lifted her face, her eyes pleading, "my friends insist that it works."

"Your friends mistake the restorative powers of nature for the fulfillment of the claims of Christian Science. After all, the Scientist's method of treatment is to go to bed and either make their own affirmations or have a practitioner make them. And, as you have seen nature cure an animal when he is quiet, so nature sometimes cures these people when they are quiet. They falsely attribute the healing to Christian Science. And if it doesn't work, they blame themselves, saying they let doubt creep in."

"But our friends, the Brooks ——"

Bev anxiously worried — what would the doctor say about Mrs. Brooks' death? Surely he couldn't blame it on Science. Thelma had said she died because they took her to the hospital.

The doctor walked to the bedroom door and back. Then, with a frown, he replied, "Mrs. Brooks was a typical example of Christian Science neglect.

At the last moment I was called in by Mr. Brooks. His wife had been run down and ailing for over a year. She developed pneumonia. I ordered her taken to the hospital, but it was too late."

"But it won't be too late for Jack, will it?"

Bev waited, fearful.

Dr. Robb weighed his words. "We can hope. If he had been at the hospital, the red streak would have been noticed by one of the nurses or myself and I would have given him penicillin. That could have licked the septicemia even a few days ago. Now, we can only hope."

Bev pushed by the doctor, crossed the room and stared through the doorway at her brother's still form. So, the red streak had been a danger signal!

Harris rose and said, "Thanks, doctor. I know you'll do all you can. It's my own fault for letting my wife talk me into trying this Christian Science."

"Men have been letting their wives talk them into things since the time of Adam," Dr. Robb answered with a kindly smile. "I'll send a nurse and be back in a couple of hours."

"Thank you," said Harris as he opened the door for the doctor.

As soon as the door closed behind Dr. Robb, Bev blurted out, "What happened?"

Mrs. Harris brushed by Bev into the bedroom and began sobbing. Mr. Harris, looking serious, explained, "Jack is worse. Mother finally became so worried over him that she was afraid she couldn't work this Christian Science stuff and phoned me at work. As soon as I got home, I phoned the doctor.

He came immediately and says blood poisoning set in too long ago."

Bev went to the doorway and stared at her brother's ashen gray face. He lay so still! If only she had told her father about the red streak! Tears came to her eyes. Her Dad put his hands on her shoulders to steady her and pleaded, "Come now, don't cry. You've got to be brave, for Mother's sake."

Be brave! How often the words rang through Bev's mind during the long, fearful hours! For a while she sat by Jack's bedside, hoping he might open his eyes, or that there might be any slight chance for the better. But his breath came in great convulsive gasps that shook the bed. Other times she had to put her hand on his chest to feel his heart beat.

She prayed a thousand frantic prayers and thought of all the bitter, accusing things she would say to Thelma the next time she saw her. Then, with a feeling of frustration, she knew it would be in vain to talk to Thelma. She would only withdraw into her icy casing. Thelma had even lost her mother and still she clung to the false hope of Christian Science!

The nurse, Miss Simpson, arrived. In her nylon uniform, she moved around the room like an efficient wraith. The lack of treatment or medicine, the fact that the nurse did almost nothing for Jack made Bev feel as if he were already beyond the ability of anyone to help him. And the nurse's square, expressionless face gave Bev the feeling that she was concealing too, too much.

Later, Dr. Robb returned, gave Mrs. Harris a sedative and sent her to bed. After he left, Bev slipped on the rose-colored robe that Jack had given her for Christmas, and dropped onto the divan by her father. She patted the folds of the robe in place. Jack had said she looked "sharp" in it. Now he didn't even know she was wearing it. Tears came to her eyes and she wiped them away with the bottom of the robe.

The night hours passed. Bev and her Dad talked long and earnestly about Jack and his illness. She felt it was one of the few times in her life that she saw beneath her Dad's blustery manner and understood how deeply he loved them all.

"Bev, I want you to get this straight," he told her. "This has been a mess about Jack. Maybe we'll lose him. I hope not, but if we do, Mother must never reproach herself. She was tricked by that quack Christian Science and her mother-heart."

Bev nodded, "I too was taken in by the false promises."

"If Jack goes, then our responsibility is to Mother. We have to convince her that God knows His business and Bev, even though it's hard sometimes to see it, I still think He does. Now, promise me you'll keep a stiff upper lip."

"Yes, Dad," Beverly promised. Of course, she must try to comfort her Mom but her conscience accused, *If I had told Mom about seeing the red streak, Jack wouldn't be this bad.*

Miss Simpson stepped to the doorway. "I think we'd better phone Dr. Robb."

Bev jumped to her feet alarmed. "No!"

"Steady now, Bev! Remember!" Harris gripped

her shoulder so tightly that he hurt her. "You call him, Miss Simpson."

Bev started toward the bedroom but Miss Simpson held up her hand, warning, "I don't think you'd better go in until the doctor arrives."

Bev dropped back on the couch to wait long dragging minutes until the doctor arrived. Her Dad paced the floor. When Dr. Robb arrived, he and Harris went into Jack's room while Bev waited more crawling minutes until her father told her what her heart already knew. Jack was gone! She didn't cry but sat there, gripping her hands tightly together.

Her Dad and the doctor went to tell her Mom while Bev waited in accusing pain. *It's all my fault!* Yet she dare say nothing to anyone. Her mother must not know that Jack might have lived if they had not been deceived by the false promises of Christian Science. If — if — if — Bev wanted to shriek, to cry, but the dreadful part of her punishment was that she had to bear her guilt alone. She must be silent for her mother's sake, so she wouldn't grieve too deeply. Bev sat numb and dry-eyed, staring at the closed bedroom door.

When the doctor and her Dad came back into the living room, Dr. Robb explained, "Miss Simpson will stay with your mother a day or two. As long as she is needed. And I'll look in on her tomorrow. Meanwhile, you'll arrange for the services?"

"Yes, thank you, Dr. Robb. I'll take care of everything," Harris answered in a husky voice.

"Call me whenever you need me," the doctor encouraged.

"Yes, Doctor," Mr. Harris muttered mechanically.

The doctor looked from Mr. Harris to Bev as if he wished there was something he could do or say to comfort them. But as there was not, he left.

When Mr. Harris was alone with his daughter, he puzzled, "Who can we get to take charge of the funeral? I suppose I can look in the phone book and get a mortuary that will know a minister to suggest."

Appealing to a stranger seemed so cold! Bev bit her lip. Who could they ask to conduct Jack's funeral? Why hadn't she gone to church or Sunday school with him? At least part of the time. But she hadn't. But he had gone to the same church as Grace. Maybe she could help. Hopefully, she suggested, "I'll phone Grace. You know, she's the girl I borrowed the Bible from."

"All right, ask her, but I think you'd better wait until morning, perhaps until six and she is awake."

"Maybe," Bev agreed, remembering that the rest of the world was asleep, that they alone were awake to grieve.

Harris crossed to the window and raised the shade. Bev stood beside him, staring out at the city street. Her heart was empty with loneliness. Never again could she go to Jack with her troubles and hear him murmur, "That's too bad, sis." Never again would she be proud when he got high marks at school or played on the winning team. A real part of herself was gone forever!

Gradually the buildings took shape in the gray light of dawn. Here and there a light flashed on in a window as someone rose early. Bev waited until the electric clock said exactly six o'clock and then she dialed Grace's number.

When Grace answered the phone it was hard for Bev to put her grief into words. She faltered, "Grace, Jack's gone!"

"I'm so sorry," Grace exclaimed warmly.

"We don't know what to do about the funeral. You know, no one but Jack went to church around here. And so ———"

"Pastor Lynch will help. I know he will."

"I'm not too sure," Bev faltered as she remembered how abruptly she had treated the man when he had tried to help. She explained, "He phoned and wanted to see Jack but I told him not to come, that Jack was too sick. He won't be mad?"

"No, dear, he won't. He'll understand. I'll phone him right away."

"Then please do." Relieved, Bev hung up.

She went into the kitchen to make coffee, but she was so upset she spilled water on the floor, and coffee on the table. Miss Simpson came out and with a too-obvious cheerfulness, helped Bev. The nurse's smile seemed to mock Bev. *She doesn't really like me.* She felt as if Miss Simpson knew she had seen the red streak and was inwardly accusing her. And when the coffee began to percolate, it sputtered, *You did it! You did it! You did it!* Bev flew into the living room and flung herself on the divan. Her sense of guilt was greater than she could stand.

There was a quick tap on the door. Harris opened it and a man said, "I'm Charles Lynch. Grace Grant asked me to come over."

"Yes, please come in," Harris invited.

Bev sat up straight and listened while her Dad

talked to the minister. Bev wasn't sure what she thought a minister should look like but she knew Mr. Lynch didn't look it. He was sort of ordinary looking, on the stocky side with a reddish-flushed face, but he had blue eyes that looked kind when he talked. And of course he, if anyone, knew about death and things like that. *Can he tell me where Jack is now? Can he tell me how to find forgiveness for the terrible thing I've done?*

She waited, every nerve on edge while the men talked about Jack's death. When they seemed finished, she blurted out, "Do you know where my brother is now?"

5: "A WAY WHICH SEEMS RIGHT" (Proverbs 14:12)

Pastor Lynch leaned toward Bev, his florid face seeming even redder with pleasure, as, in a warm voice he assured her, "I'm thankful that I have good news for you about Jack. You know he'd been going to our high school department of late. He even talked to me about being baptized, and I know from talks with him that he believed, that he was saved."

Saved! Bev thought. *What does he mean by that? Is it something to do with that kind of happy way Jack had of late? Maybe Mr. Lynch means that Jack has gone to heaven for sure! I'd like to ask him a million questions but I can't today!*

She sat there listening quietly while the minister and her father made several phone calls, arranging for the funeral while her heart accused, over and over again, *I'm to blame for Jack's death. I'm to blame!*

All that day and the next, Bev went around the apartment feeling so guilty it was hard to be brave in front of her mother. Somehow, she managed and she wondered if Thelma didn't feel the way as she did — desperate inside but hard outside. Maybe Thelma even kept on trying to make Science work so she wouldn't feel that her believing in it made her responsible for her mother's death. She was doing anything in an effort to still her conscience! Bev felt as if at last she understood Thelma and her cold detached manner. She was trying to keep from thinking!

The morning of the funeral, the activity helped Bev to forget her grief part of the time. Miss Simpson, the nurse, insisted that the family eat breakfast. A potted hyacinth arrived from the Grants. Miss Simpson put it in Jack's room and when Bev passed by the door, the flower was a bright spot in the gloom.

Miss Simpson helped Mrs. Harris dress while Bev put on the only good dress that she had that was a dark color. It was a sharp navy blue, full-skirted, taffeta, but at least it was dark and suitable for a funeral.

She went with her parents to the church and there, the Reverend Lynch ushered them to the front row. The coffin, almost directly in front of her, was banked with flowers. The bright pinks and yellows somehow softened the sight of her happy Jack, lying so still and quiet.

Pastor Lynch announced that Jack's favorite gospel song would be sung. A trio of young girls, slightly older than Bev, sang, "It Took a Miracle," and Bev remembered how delightedly Jack had played the record over and over again. The song made her feel almost as if he were alive again.

Then Pastor Lynch stood in the pulpit and began reading scripture. "I am the resurrection and the life. He that believeth in me, though he were dead, yet shall he live."

"Yet shall he live," echoed in Bev's heart and a feeling of peace filled her. She thought, *How wonderful that Jack is still alive, some place! He must be. This isn't like Science which only a few believe. Why nearly everyone in the world believes that we have a soul which goes on living after we die.*

"I am the way, the truth ———" the minister continued.

Bev remembered the day Grace and Thelma had disagreed about Jesus being the Way or the Way-shower. Grace had been right. If only she had listened to Grace! She must talk to her again. Maybe she would know some way she could find relief from her burden of guilt. Bev listened hopefully as the minister read verse after verse from the Bible. *Scientists read both the Bible and "Science and Health," but they put "Science and Health" first. But from now on I'm going to read only the Bible.*

At the close of the service, when her friends walked by the casket, Bev saw Grace, Nadine and several other friends from school. But not Thelma. Bev knew why. Thelma would say Bev had given in to mortal error and allowed her brother to die. Thelma could be cruel!

Andy and Clyde, who had been in the accident with Jack, and their parents, walked by. If it hadn't been for Science Jack would still be alive, as Andy and Clyde were! Bev squeezed her handkerchief in a tight ball and blinked back her tears. Her grief was hard to bear!

When the service was over and the family was home again, Bev had a let-down feeling. Life had to go on without Jack! Miss Simpson left and Mrs. Harris helped Bev back into her own room. And the next day Mr. Harris went back to work, while Bev and her mother packed Jack's clothes to give them to a charitable organization.

Mrs. Harris kept his little trinkets and Bev kept his books. She wasn't surprised to find a Bible among them. It was an inexpensive one and almost new but in the Gospel of John a number of verses were underlined with red. He must have enjoyed reading it. She remembered the times he had tried to talk religion to her and she hadn't been interested. Well, she was interested now!

The first day Bev was back at school, Grace joined her on the 'Aud' steps at lunchtime. Grace's oval face brimmed with sympathy when she said, "I'm so sorry, Bev, but we must trust that God is always right and that He was right when He took Jack to heaven."

"I suppose so. You know, Grace, I'm going to start going to some church. I want to know about religion."

"Not about religion, Bev! You want to know about the Lord Jesus!"

Bev frowned. Grace was making a distinction between religion and Jesus that she didn't understand. Someone tapped her on the shoulder and Bev glanced up.

"I've something special to tell you," Nadine said in a hushed, important tone.

Bev murmured, "Excuse me," to Grace and strolled across the grounds with Nadine. Nadine opened her black eyes wide and in a solemn voice asked, "Would you like to talk to your brother?"

Startled, Bev stopped still, the color draining from her face, "What do you mean?"

"Spiritualism! Don't you remember? I told you about it. It really has all the answers. The last few weeks Mom and I have been going to the spiritualist church and the medium gives messages from the living dead. The other night, we had a message from Dad."

"Tell me," Bev insisted. The thought of actually talking to Jack was exciting!

"Well, Rose Parker, she's the medium, she told Mom that a middle-aged man was standing right behind her. Mom instantly recognized him as Dad. Mrs. Parker said that he said for Mom not to grieve, that he was happy in the spiritland and that she would soon make an investment that would make her a lot of money."

"How wonderful! You must take Mom and me."

"I'm sure my Mom would like to have you go with us," Nadine said. "That's why I told you."

The bell rang with Bev promising to see Nadine after school. Then Bev went to her class. She fretted, *Why do I have to go to school as if nothing had happened when everything is happening?*

When classes were over, Grace came to Bev's desk and invited, "Bev, would you like to come to church with me Sunday?"

Bev drew her eyebrows together in a slight frown. She hated to say no, but she knew that at Grace's church no one talked with the dead. She shook her head and answered, "I'm sorry but I've promised to go to Nadine's church."

"Oh!" Grace looked wilted.

Bev walked briskly to where Nadine was waiting for her on the front steps of the building. As they walked down the street, Nadine told Bev more of her mother's disappointment in Science and other cults, but she gleefully concluded, "Bev, now we've found the real thing."

"I hope so! It will mean so much to my Mom."

The girls trotted up the stairs to the Harris's apartment. Bev opened the door and called, "Hi, Mom."

The smell of spicy molasses cookies filled the living room and Bev realized that her Mom was baking cookies for the first time since the accident. She knew she was trying to be brave. Bev led Nadine into the kitchen.

"Hello girls," Mrs. Harris glanced up from cutting cookies. "Have one." She waved her hand toward a row of baked cookies.

Bev took a bite and explained, "Mom, Nadine knows a church where we can talk to Jack."

Mrs. Harris dropped the cookie cutter with a clatter, and in a frightened tone, asked, "What do you mean?"

Nadine quickly gulped her cookie and then, in her friendly way, told of her visit to the spiritualist church.

Tears came to Mrs. Harris's eyes. She clung to Bev and sobbed, "We must try. We must"

"You can go with Mom and me," Nadine assured her.

After she left, Mrs. Harris rolled the rest of the cookie dough and put it in the refrigerator. She explained, "I'm too upset to bake any more. We'll just have scrambled eggs for dinner."

"Sure, Mom, that's enough," Bev agreed, not wanting her mother to work when she was so upset. And how could she help but be excited at the thought of actually talking to the dead!

The phone rang, and wondering who it might be, Bev stepped into the small hall, picked up the phone and said, "Hello."

"Good afternoon," came a deep voice that Bev instantly recognized as Pastor Lynch. She could hear again as he read scripture verses at Jack's funeral. "I was wondering if your mother was home. I thought I'd drop over."

He always phones at the wrong time. If he comes now he might persuade Mom not to go to the medium and I want to talk to Jack. I have to, to see if he forgives me. She said, "I'm sorry but mother is too upset to see anyone yet."

"But perhaps I could say a word or two of comfort."

His persistency alarmed Bev and she insisted, "I said she didn't want to see anyone."

"Well, she knows how she feels, but should she feel better, I'd be happy to come over."

"If she does, I'll let you know. Good-by."

"Good-by." There was a slight pause, then the click of the receiver. Relieved Bev hung up.

Mrs. Harris called, "Who was that, dear?"

Bev hesitated, wondering how she could explain to her mother what she'd done, so her mother would agree that she'd been right. "Oh, it was that minister who preached Jack's funeral. He wanted to come over but you know those old fashioned churches don't really know anything."

"I'm not too sure," Mrs. Harris objected.

"But Mom. You do want to actually talk to Jack, don't you?"

"Of course, only, well, it was kind of the minister to call anyway."

"Yes, it was kind," Bev agreed, and went to her room. *Only I want to actually talk to Jack, if I at all can!* She changed her dress and did homework until her father arrived. Then she helped her mother with the dinner, all the time hoping that her father would be in an agreeable mood and not object too much to what they wanted to do.

Mrs. Harris waited, as usual, until her husband was through eating, then told him of her new hopes.

"Honey," he objected, "I think going to a place like that will only keep your grief an open wound."

Mrs. Harris's face was thin and tired as she pleaded, "Tom, I must try. I must."

"We must, Dad," Bev insisted. *He doesn't understand that I must know if Jack thinks I've killed him!*

"All right," he agreed. And she realized that because of her mother's grief, her father hadn't objected as much as he once would have.

"I want you to do anything you think will make you happy, but I don't think there is anything in this spirit stuff."

Bev smiled with relief. Everything would work out all right. Only she thought she couldn't wait until

Wednesday. She and her mother planned how carefully they would be not to tell the medium anything about themselves. Mrs. Harris reminded, "Your Dad says these women are smart fakers, and we mustn't be deceived."

Not again! Oh no, not again!

Wednesday night, when the Lockwoods came, Bev and her mother were ready to go. As they walked down the stairs to the street, Bev decided that Mrs. Lockwood had been as pretty as Nadine when she was younger. She had heavy black hair, large dark eyes, but her face was so thin and her mouth drooped. It distressed Bev to see the woman looking so troubled. *If the spiritualist religion is right it ought to make her happy, but obviously it hasn't.*

Bev was so preoccupied that she tripped and Mrs. Harris had to catch her arm to steady her. Bev's heart grew sad as she thought, *Isn't there any real comfort in any religion?*

6: "TREES WHOSE FRUIT WITHERS" (Jude 12)

WHEN THE HARRISES AND LOCKWOODS arrived at the spiritualist church, Bev was surprised because it did not look dark and mysterious. It was merely a large frame house and the meeting was held in a living room and dining room which opened into each other. The blue striped wallpaper was faded and the figured carpet was worn. At the far end of the room was an upright piano and a small table. The congregation consisted of middle-aged women with sad faces, a sprinkling of men, and a few smart-looking young people, sitting on folding chairs.

A slight, wispy man drummed out a hymn and the people sang. A woman came in and stood up at the front, resting her fingertips on the table. Nadine nudged Bev, "That's the medium, Rose Parker."

Again Bev felt disappointed. Rose Parker was an ordinary-looking woman, stout, with henna-colored hair. Her ill-fitting dress was of a large flowery pattern and her white slip showed at the back. She talked about hope, making vague promises that all would be well someday. As she talked, she kept wiping her hands on her handkerchief.

Then she closed her eyes, bent her head to one

side as if she were listening, stretched out her arms as if she were trying to reach someone and began giving messages. She told of the different people she saw and what they said and Bev was fascinated.

The medium bent her head a little lower and in a hesitating voice said, "There is a new spirit here tonight. One who has just passed beyond. He is trying to contact someone. He is hovering over that lady in the third row. The one with pink flowers on her hat."

Bev gasped — the medium meant her mother! Mrs. Harris began to sob quietly, but her face looked hopeful. Bev squeezed her mother's hand.

"I can't see the figure as clearly as I would like to. Whoever he is, he doesn't know how to manifest himself. But he gives this message. He says, 'Mom, do not grieve. I'm happy.'"

Then the medium started giving a message to someone else. Bev held her Mom's cold hand in hers and marvelled that Rose Parker could tell that her brother had died recently. *Perhaps this is it!* Hope mounted in her heart!

Bev and her mother were so pleased with the message that every Wednesday and Sunday night they went to the meetings. The next time Rose Parker saw the spirit clearly enough to tell that he was good-looking and, at still another meeting, she told them that he had died suddenly. But the evening meeting was fairly well attended and Mrs. Harris did not receive a message each time she went.

She was so disappointed when she did not receive a message that she began going to a smaller

Friday afternoon meeting. At it, a set charge was made and every one received a message. When she came home from one of those meetings she was cheerful and happy for an hour or so, then she would go into her room and cry.

"I don't like it," Mr. Harris complained. "Those meetings act like dope. They give her a false cheer and when the reaction sets in, she feels worse than ever."

Bev nodded sadly and began carrying the dishes from the table to the sink. She wasn't satisfied either with the meetings. They weren't accomplishing all she had hoped they would. She wanted to ask her brother a question. Instead, Rose Parker was always vague in the messages she claimed came from Jack.

Harris strolled into the living room and Bev stacked the dishes into the automatic dishwasher. It seemed as if what Rose Parker told them, she could tell anyone. In fact, she said almost the same thing to everyone. Perhaps she hadn't really contacted Jack! True she had told Mom she lost a son, but hadn't everyone who went to her meetings lost someone?

Bev put down the top and flipped the switch. The hum of the dishwasher made sort of a background for her thoughts going round and round. . . . How did Rose Parker know her Mom had lost a son? She could have lost her father. Perhaps the medium just sensed it, as sometimes Bev sensed things before her Mom told her. Bev shook her head. It was too deep for her.

The next day she was still troubled about Rose Parker and her messages when Nadine suggested,

"Bev, Mom is trying to get a group together for a special materialization meeting. Would you and your mother be interested in coming?"

"What is it?"

"It's very special. Mrs. Parker only allows a small group to attend. She goes into a trance and the spirits materialize with ectoplasm."

"You mean you can actually see the spirits?"

"Yes," Nadine nodded earnestly.

"Then count us in. I'm sure Mom will want to go."

This, at last, is something definite! Bev told Mrs. Harris about the special meeting and she phoned Mrs. Lockwood arranging to go. When Mrs. Harris explained about the special meeting to Mr. Harris, he narrowed his eyes, then decided, "Sounds interesting! I'll go with you."

Bev glanced at him with surprise. *Whatever made Dad willing to go? Had he decided it might be the truth?* She didn't know why he was going but she felt relieved because he was.

The meeting was held on a Friday night. The sliding door closing off the dining room was shut and the small group gathered in the front room of Rose Parker's home. Only the Harrises, Lockwoods and two other families whom Beverly had seen often at the meetings, were there. Mr. Walker, a stout, ample-chinned man, was the only man besides Harris. The two sat together near the door while Bev and her mother sat near the front.

One corner of the room was curtained off. The black curtain, hung on a cat-corner wire, was about five feet high. Mrs. Parker announced that her husband, a scrawny man who always held his head to one side, would take charge of the meeting. With a business-like gesture, she pulled aside the curtain, showing that there was nothing behind it but a straight chair; then she stepped inside and Mr. Parker fussed with the curtains.

Then he turned to the group and with close, birdlike movements he led them in singing, "Shall we gather at the river?" After the doleful singing he eased around the chairs, going to the door and click-ing the light switch. Bev shivered in the darkness. The group in slow dragging tones began singing, "Lead Kindly Light."

Bev felt as if the darkness had weight and was pushing her down, down. One by one the singers stopped and everyone was so quiet Bev could hear her mother's strained breathing.

A moan drifted across the room.

"Rose is going under," Mr. Parker said in a hushed artificial whisper.

Mrs. Harris sobbed and clung to Bev. A light wavered and flickered in mid-air.

"Someone is trying to materialize," Mr. Parker cautioned. "Be still."

The light glowed and grew larger and larger.

"Beverly ——— Beverly ———" came a low cry from the corner.

"Jack," Mrs. Harris screamed.

The lights flashed on with almost blinding sud-denness. Bev caught a glimpse of a cloth being pulled over the top of the curtain.

"Who did that?" Mr. Parker demanded in a squeaky, exasperated voice.

Harris, standing by the door, in an indignant voice admitted, "I switched on the lights. You two parasites prey on the grief of women, deceiving them. That was no spirit, only Mrs. Parker standing on the chair, waving a rag covered with phosphorus paint."

Mrs. Parker stepped from behind the curtain, her eyes blazing and the lines criss-crossed on her face with anger. She shouted, "Get out of here, all of you! I try to help and you trick me, setting a spy near the switch. Get out of here, I say, and never come back!"

"Believe me, we will and gladly." Harris strode toward Bev and her mother and tried to hurry them out of the room. Some of the people moved toward the door, others stood around excitedly talking. Mrs. Parker kept shrieking "Get out of here! Get out of here!"

Out on the street, Mr. Harris explained to Mr. Walker, "I wanted to show my wife she'd been duped but I don't want to make Mrs. Parker any trouble. It would be too hard on Mrs. Harris to be a witness at a trial."

"I feel the same way," Mr. Walker nodded in sort of helpless agreement. "That's why I came along tonight, but it's because none of us want trouble that this so-called medium gets by with deceiving one poor soul after another."

"The police will catch up with her in time," Harris assured the man.

So it was all a fake, Bev thought, feeling almost as low and discouraged as she had when Jack died.

With flagging footsteps Bev followed her Dad and
Mother to the car. She was beyond caring what happened to Rose Parker. She was too down-hearted to
care about anything.

She still felt low when, the next day at school
during lunch period, Nadine said, "Mother and I certainly aren't going to Rose Parker's any more."

"Who is?" Bev replied sadly.

"She'll get some new ones. But Mom has been
dissatisfied for some time. When you listen real close,
Rose Parker never really says anything definite, so
Mom has decided to study reincarnation."

"Reincarnation?"

"You know. They believe when we die, we come
back to this earth in another body. That would ac-
count for the difference in people's lives. Those who
are poor and sick are really suffering for sins they com-
mitted in a former life."

"Oh, no!" Bev's face turned white. It was bad
enough to suffer for her sins in this life, without being born another time to suffer again for them!

7: "JOY IN THE MORNING" (Psalm 30:5)

BEV WALKED AWAY FROM NADINE
as quickly as she could. The thought of suffering for
her sins in still another life was too much! If only
she didn't feel responsible for Jack's death. If only——
She had too many "if's" and no answers to them.

She walked down the hall and went inside the
classroom. It was empty but for Miss Mackintosh
eating a banana while she corrected papers.

Bev paused at Grace's desk. Grace hadn't been
to school for several days. Why? She walked up the
aisle. "Miss Mackintosh, do you know why Grace is
absent?"

Miss Mackintosh looked up, carefully keeping
her finger on her place. "She has rheumatic fever and
will have to stay in bed for months, that is, several
months."

"Oh!" With a feeling of shock and sadness, Bev
tried to picture Grace, with her sweet, friendly ways,
sick in bed. Poor, poor Grace! How upset and worried
her mother must be! How unhappy Grace must be!

Later, after school, Bev decided to go see her
friend. She ought to return the Bible anyway. She
hadn't read it for a long time, not since she had been
going to the spiritualist meetings. She went home,

explained to her Mom where she was going and, with the Bible, walked the few blocks to Grace's.

Grace lived in a small house in the rear of an apartment house. The yard was tidy, but the frame house was in need of paint, plainly showing that the Grants were poor.

Bev stepped onto the small porch, rang the bell, and waited anxiously. She almost dreaded seeing someone who was sick. She didn't know a thing comforting to say!

The door opened and Mrs. Grant, in a blue striped dress and flowered apron, said, "Hello, Bev."

Her smile reminded Bev of Grace. She had the same sweet expression around the mouth and the same happy light in her eyes. Her cheerful manner made Bev feel better and she decided that Grace couldn't be too sick if her mother was this cheerful. Bev explained, "I heard Grace was sick and came to see her."

"She'll be pleased to see you. The days are rather long for her."

Bev followed Mrs. Grant through the living room, a trifle old-fashioned, but brightened by a bowl of daffodils, into the bedroom. It was a pleasant room, with blue-flowered wallpaper and white painted furniture. In the bed, under a blue puff comforter, was Grace. She smiled, "Hi, Bev."

"Hi. I brought back your Bible." Bev put the Bible on the small table near the bed. She thought she had never seen Grace look prettier. She had on a pink, quilted bed jacket and her sandy hair was combed softly around her face. "You sure don't look sick!"

"She's content and that's the most important thing," Mrs. Grant said. "If you need me, call me." She smiled at the girls and left the room.

"Pull up a chair, Bev," Grace invited.

Bev pulled up an old wicker chair, sat down and stared at Grace. She couldn't get over how happy her friend looked. "I thought when Miss Mackintosh said you had rheumatic fever that you were real sick."

"The doctor says I'll have to stay in bed for several months, and that it may be a long time before I'm strong."

"But you don't look unhappy. Why?"

"It was disappointing at first," Grace admitted. "But I prayed and decided I couldn't really be unhappy and complain when I had Jesus."

"Jesus!" Beverly repeated and slumped down into the chair. "I've heard a lot about Him but I can't say that I know anything about Him that would keep me from being unhappy."

"But He would make you happy if you knew Him as Saviour. Bev, I can't invite you to come to church with me because I can't go, but you know Pastor Lynch. He'd like to see you there, I'm sure."

"I'm not at all sure he would. He phoned several times wanting to see mother, but we were so busy he finally quit calling. Besides, I'm never going to another church in my life."

"Bev, don't say that!"

"You would too if you'd been through all I have," and Bev told of the phoney spiritualist seance. "Re-

ligion's just a fake. Science didn't work when we put
it to a test and there's nothing to spiritualism."

"Bev, dear, you're disappointed because you try
religions instead of going to the Lord Himself. Why
do you go to those cults?"

Bev sighed. Dear, sweet Grace would never understand the burden of her heart! "I had to go some
place. I was hunting something."

"Only Jesus satisfies!"

"But every church claims Jesus."

"I suppose they sound alike to you but there is
a difference. Those cults quote some of the wise things
that the Lord Jesus said but a church where you can
really find Jesus is one that tells about His Cross and
that He saves."

"Saves!" Bev exclaimed. "That's what Pastor
Lynch had said about Jack; that he was saved! What
do you mean by 'saved'?"

"That we're all sinners, every one of us, and that
Christ died on the Cross to save us from our sins.
When we believe in Him as Saviour, we're saved, we
belong to Jesus."

Bev smiled faintly at the idea of belonging to
Jesus. It would be wonderful to think someone cared
for her. Then she faltered, "But how can I ever believe in any religion again?"

"If you will try believing in Jesus as hard as you
did those other religions, I'm sure the Lord will prove
Himself to you as He has to me."

A spark of hope came into Bev's heart. She knew
that any real help she'd had, had come from Grace.
She had loaned her Bible when she needed it. She had

sent Pastor Lynch to her home to arrange for the funeral. And he had tried to be kind. Too, now that Grace was sick, she was as brave and happy as ever. But then she hadn't done anything wrong like she had. Bev explained, "But, Grace, you don't understand. I need Jack's forgiveness for something I did."

Grace leaned toward her, an excited light on her face. "Bev, it wouldn't do you any good to have Jack forgive you anything you'd done. He's only a human being, the same as you are. If you've done something wrong, then you need God's forgiveness."

Bev took a deep breath as she realized, "That's true!"

"If you'll only believe in Jesus, He will forgive you."

"Believe what?"

"For one thing, you must believe that He is the Son of God. The Bible says, 'Whoever shall confess that Jesus is the Son of God, God dwelleth in him.' "

"The Son of God," Bev repeated.

"Yes, for 'The Father sent the Son to be the Saviour of the world,' and 'as many as received him to them gave he the power to become the sons of God, even to them that believe on his name.' "

"It seems too good to be true!"

"And the Lord will comfort your Mom. He says, 'Come unto me all ye that labour and are heavy laden, and I will give you rest.' "

Bev's heart was awed by the greatness of God's promises. And she knew Grace was right. She had tried the other religions — why not try believing in Jesus as Saviour? "What do I do?"

"Kneel, ask Jesus to forgive your sins and come into your heart so you can live for Him."

Bev's burden of guilt seemed to push her to her knees beside the bed. She closed her eyes and felt Grace's warm hand on hers. She tried to find words to tell God that she wanted to believe in Christ, but she didn't know what to say. She knew she should tell Him she had been wrong to try those false religions. Suddenly, she sobbed, forgetting everything, asking the Lord to forgive her and show her what to do.

A hush filled the room. Bev dabbed her eyes with her handkerchief and then she realized that there was peace in her heart. "Why, Grace, I feel better. I don't know what happened but I feel all clean inside."

"It is Jesus," Grace said in a happy tone of voice. "I'll tell Pastor Lynch, and this time you will see him won't you? And go to church?"

"Oh, yes, gladly." Bev stood up, smiling. Then, seeing the Bible where she had put it, she said, "I won't have to borrow your Bible back again because I have my brother's. I want to read it."

"You must. Read everything in it that Jesus said!"

Bev nodded and held the Bible close, realizing that in it and in the Lord Jesus she had found the answer to all her questions. Her heart was satisfied!

NOTE: All quotations from *Science and Health*, 1915 Edition.

Page 18 — see pages 468 and 493
Page 21 — see page 591

Page 24 — see pages 107 and 108
Page 26 — see page 297
Page 41 — see page 468

All quotes from Holy Bible.

Page 73 — I John 4:15, I John 4:14, John 1:12 and Matthew 11:28.

Prior Publication:

"Beverly's Quest" was published originally in *Our Young People,* printed by Augsburg Publishing House.

As "Beverly Sees It Through" in the *Sunday School Messenger,* published by Pilgrim Publishing House.

As "An Answer for Beverly" in *Companion,* published by the Mennonite Publishing House.

A PERSONAL TESTIMONY

THE AUTHOR'S PERSONAL EXPERIENCE

THOUGH I GREW UP IN THE UNITED STATES, I was as much a heathen as any savage in darkest Africa. My mother's parents had been Protestant and, after an unsuccessful marriage, she was attracted by the promises of the cults which flourished in so-called Christian America.

My earliest religious memory is walking down the street, when I was about eight years old, repeating the "Scientific Statement of Being." When other children were learning the Lord's prayer and the twenty-third Psalm, I was taught, "There is no life, truth, intelligence nor substance in matter. All is infinite Mind and its infinite manifestations, for God is All-in-all. Spirit is the real and eternal, matter is the unreal and temporal. Spirit is God and Man is His image and likeness, therefore man is not material, he is spiritual" (*Science and Health with Key to the Scriptures* by Mary Baker Eddy, page 468).

I repeated these sentences because I was afraid of Animal Magnetism. Mother sent me to the Christian Science Sunday school and though the teachers taught the nothingness of matter, they also taught that it could hurt me unless I repeated the Scientific Statement of

Being often enough. I used to walk down the street, repeating it over and over so no automobile or disease germ could hurt me. I was taught to trust the repeating of it the same as a savage chants a meaningless phrase over and over again to ward off evil spirits.

Mother went from Christian Science to Unity, to Theosophy, to Numerology, to Astrology, with a dash of Palmistry, Reincarnation and finally Spiritualism.

In Unity she was hopeful for awhile, but she soon found it to be merely a modified form of Christian Science. It didn't bring her the health, peace and prosperity it promised.

Theosophy and related metaphysics absorbed her for many years, making her a morbid, brooding, unhappy woman. I reflected her state of mind, becoming in my late teens a depressed, fear-bound girl.

Numerology laid all our unhappiness to the fact that we were both incorrectly named. She changed both our first names which caused confusion for many years. Numerology changed our names, but not our lives or our hearts.

Palmistry proved to be a fatalistic method of fortune telling and while it interested my young mind, it offered no real help. After buying and studying many books on Palmistry we gave it up.

I think Astrology was the worst. For years mother lived by her chart. If the day were an ill-omened day on the chart, she would not even use the telephone nor bake a cake. She would remain in bed writing letters or reading more metaphysics. We would keep the house dark, and I usually read a dramatic novel, for though her beliefs overshadowed my life, making it a dark and mystic thing, I was too young to spend the day struggling through the mental calisthenics of these cults.

If the day were not bad because of the astrology, it was bad because of her dreams. She lived with a dream book by her bedside. Before breakfast she looked up the meanings of the dreams she had in the night. If she had dreamed something bad, we lived in dread until we received evil tidings. If she dreamed of someone dead, she expected to hear from the living and we watched for the mailman. She had only one dream that brought good luck. How relieved I was when she occasionally dreamed that!

Every detail of my life was bound by superstition. If I forgot something when I left the house and had to come back for it, I had to go through the ritual of walking around a chair three times and sitting down in three chairs for three minutes each to break the spell so I would not have the bad luck. What house-keeping I was taught was in reality a series of good luck taboos, no shoes on a shelf higher than one's head, no umbrella open in the house, no hat on the bed and so on. All day long my actions were checked by the luck they would or would not bring. Fear was my constant companion.

Mother's one sign of good luck was when her left hand itched. It meant we would receive money. Perhaps I would get work, or she would, or we would receive some of the ever over-due alimony. I used to think I would be really grown up when my own hand would itch and I could foretell good luck. I waited vainly for that day. My hand never seemed to itch at the right time. Mother told me that the power would not pass to me until her death.

Spiritualism was mother's last cult. The first time mother and I went to a public meeting the medium said my grandmother wanted to contact us and that she carried a bird cage in her hand. This completely captivated my mother because my grandmother's name had been Bird. Surely it was the devil deluding the medium and us! After that, Mother poured out money for private sittings. We used to go to the medium's home, to the darkness of the cellar, and with others, sit around a table, singing my grandmother's favorite hymn, "Shall We Gather at the River?" But Grandmother never materialized.

How long ago that all seems! After vainly searching, believing their false claims without results, Mother, when forty-seven, shot herself in desperation. She had found nothing in life to satisfy her. The shock of her death sent me searching. I paid a Christian Scientist practitioner to tell me that my mother had become part of the Infinite. I paid a spiritualist medium to tell me Mother would wander in outer darkness until the time came when she would have died naturally. A Catholic priest suggested that I pray her out of purgatory.

Finally, weary, I telephoned a near-by church and, unwilling to hear the minister preach, I asked if they had a week-day Bible class. They had. I attended it, and was surprised to learn that just because one is born one is not a child of God. But, "As many as received him, to them gave he power to become the

sons of God, even to them that believe on his name"
(John 1:12).

My next question was, "Believe what?"

That, "All have sinned and come short of the glory
of God" (Romans 3:23).

It was not hard to search my heart, and find sin
there, but what should I do with it?

I found the answer in "That if thou shalt confess
with thy mouth the Lord Jesus, and shalt believe in
thine heart that God hath raised him from the dead,
thou shalt be saved" (Romans 10:9).

Yes, in Christ I was saved, not only from sin, but
in Him I found the answer to *all* my fears and questions.

It was the fall of 1932 when I said "I believe" and
became a new creature in Christ Jesus. Since then I
have faced the false teachings of the cults in the light
of Christ and God's Word.

Christ alone is the answer to Christian Science
because Christ acknowledged that man is not only
mind, but body. Sickness is not to be scorned because
a person has not thought correctly, but should arouse
our compassion as it did the compassion of Christ.
Neither is sin unreal, for Christ said, "That ye may
know that the Son of man hath power on earth to
forgive sins" (Matthew 9:6). As for the animal magnetism which the Christian Scientist fears, there is no
references to it in the Word of God.

Christ is the answer to the mental gymnastics of
Theosophy, because in Him "Are hid all the treasures
of wisdom and knowledge" (Colossians 2:3). Books
on Theosophy lead one through a mental labyrinth,

full of abstract terms, but the Word of God is simple, telling, often in story form, God's way for us to live.

Christ is the answer to Numerology because it is not our name, but His Name, which is important. We pray in Christ's Name and some day we will discard our name because in eternity we will be given a new name (Revelation 2:17).

Christ is the answer to Palmistry because when we become a child of God we know our future is not dependent upon the lines of our hands, but in the fact that "Even the days that were ordained for me, when as yet there was none of them" (Psalm 139:16, ARV), and that "He hath chosen us in Him before the foundation of the world" (Ephesians 1:4).

Christ is the answer to Astrology because "Thus saith the Lord, Learn not the way of the heathen and be not dismayed at the signs of heaven" (Jeremiah 10:2). In the days of my girlhood, if the stars were wrong, I faced the day with fear. Now I face each day with confidence, knowing that it is secure in Him.

Christ is the answer to Spiritualism, not because we have received a message from the dead, but because death has been conquered by One who died and rose again, by One who said, "I am the resurrection and the life" (John 11:25).

I thank Christ for freeing me from the mumbo-jumbo of heathen cults. It is a relief to get up in the morning and know that neither my name, the stars, animal magnetism, nor even the lines on my hands can affect me because "If the Son therefore shall make you free, ye shall be free indeed" (John 8:36).

Let it not be said of you, "Because they received

not the love of the truth, that they might be saved . . . For this cause God shall send them strong delusions, that they should believe a lie" (II Thessalonians 2: 10, 11), but rather, "He that heareth my word, and believeth on him that sent me, hath everlasting life, and shall not come into condemnation; but is passed from death unto life" (John 5:24).